SPIDER KANE

and the
Mystery Under
the May-Apple

by	illustrated
Mary Pope	by
Osborne	Victoria
	Chess

BULLSEYE BOOKS • ALFRED A. KNOPF
NEW YORK

For my brother, Bill — M. P. O.

To Richard and Norman, with love — V. C.

A BULLSEYE BOOK PUBLISHED BY ALFRED A. KNOPF, INC.
Copyright © 1992 by Mary Pope Osborne
Cover and interior illustrations copyright © 1992 by Victoria Chess

Grateful acknowledgment is made to Williamson Music Co. for permission to
reprint excerpts from the song "Some Enchanted Evening" by Richard Rodgers
and Oscar Hammerstein II. Copyright 1949 by Richard Rodgers and Oscar
Hammerstein II. Copyright renewed by Williamson Music Co., owner of publi-
cation and allied rights. Used by permission. All rights reserved.

Library of Congress Catalog Card Number: 90-33524
ISBN: 0-679-84174-1
RL: 5.2
First Bullseye Books edition: May 1993

Manufactured in the United States of America   10 9 8 7 6 5 4 3 2 1

New York, Toronto, London, Sydney, Auckland

The last and least of things
That soar on quivering wings,
Or crawl among the grass blades out of sight
Have just as clear a right
To their appointed portion of delight
As queens or kings.

—Christina G. Rossetti

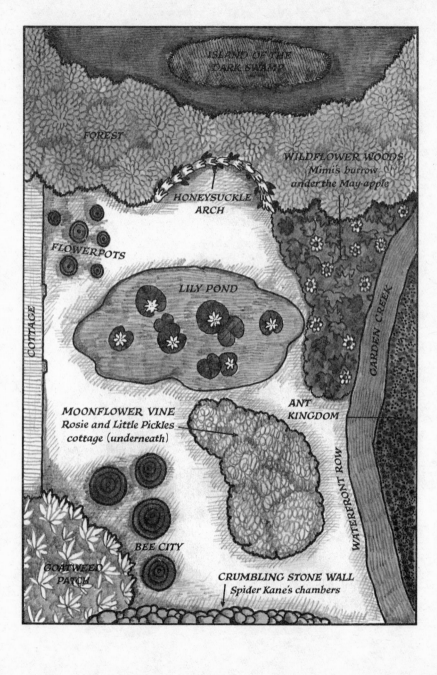

CAST OF CHARACTERS
(in Order of Appearance)

PUPA LEAFWING—A social-climbing butterfly; currently goes by name "La Mère"

LEON LEAFWING—Pupa Leafwing's son; a hotheaded, earnest young butterfly

MIMI—An attractive, gossamer-winged butterfly with a mysterious past

ROSIE—An energetic ladybug who caters for the Cottage Garden

LITTLE PICKLES—Rosie's companion; a good-natured ladybug who also caters for the Cottage Garden and makes tulip cradles for Garden babies

WALTER DOGTICK—Pupa Leafwing's former best friend; now an indigent scavenger

SPIDER KANE—Retired captain from the Mosquito Wars, theater director, jazz musician, and amateur sleuth

MIDGE APPLEWORM—A middle-aged, wealthy matron

LOU SALAMANDER
and NYMPH LATELL—Members of the Women's Bug Club

COLONEL APPLEWORM (Ret.)—Midge's husband, nicknamed "Tubby"

DR. T. K. ANT—Head librarian of the National Ant Archives

MAJOR GENERAL ROBERT
"BOB" BUM—Steward of the queen and deputy treasurer of Bee City

SERGEANT THOMAS
HAWKINS—A burned-out moth nicknamed "The Hawk"; one of the emperor's henchmen

MARGARET—Mimi's mother; an aged, gossamer-winged butterfly

EMPEROR MOTH—Ruler of the Island of the Dark Swamp

A few mosquitos; hordes of grubs

Part I

Thunder rumbled in the distance. The sky above the abandoned Cottage Garden was dark gray. As the summer breeze blew the tall weeds and flowers, tiny butterfly voices came from inside a broken geranium pot.

"There's that tacky thing again," said La Mère Leafwing, peering outside.

Leon Leafwing looked up from his book and gazed at his mother. "What tacky thing?"

"There. Over by the Appleworms' pot."

Leon squinted at the gossamer-winged butterfly hovering near Colonel and Mrs. Appleworm's flowerpot. She wore a blue iridescent gown and dark glasses. "Wow, she looks wonderful," he breathed.

"Wonderful?" La Mère snorted. "I saw her yesterday near the Lily Pond. She was embracing some horrible-looking creature. He had a red bandanna around his head and—"

"Goodness," interrupted Leon. "She dropped something—she doesn't seem to realize it. She's starting to take off—"

"Stay right where you are, dearie," said La Mère. "She's no good. I'm telling you I saw her—"

Before his mother could finish, Leon soared out of the geranium pot and zoomed over to the Appleworms'. He scooped up a tiny purple silk scarf, then darted as fast as he could after the gossamer-winged butterfly.

"Excuse me—" he called, but she didn't seem to hear him. He flew alongside her, and just as he reached out to tap her, she turned.

"Help!" she screamed, flailing her arms wildly.

Leon ducked and managed to cover his head.

"Your scarf!" he shouted. "Your scarf!"

She stopped in midair. "What?"

"You dropped your scarf!"

"Oh!" The gossamer-winged butterfly lit down in the tall meadow rue. "Goodness, were you just trying to return my scarf?" she asked, panting.

"Yes," said Leon. And he handed over the tiny piece of purple silk.

"Oh, I'm so sorry. Will you forgive me for being so stupid?"

"You're forgiven; no harm done. What's your name?"

"They call me Mimi," she said. She took off her sunglasses. And Leon saw traces of sorrow and fear in her dark, lovely eyes. "And you?"

"Leon. Leon Leafwing."

"Oh, what a good name. Leon Leafwing. It sounds so brave and reassuring."

Before Leon could speak, a clap of thunder cracked the sky.

"Help!" Mimi screamed, throwing herself into Leon's arms. She was trembling like a leaf.

"It's only thunder," he said softly.

"I'm sorry, Leon," she said. Then to his surprise, she began weeping. "But I'm so afraid . . ." she whispered.

"What are you afraid of?"

"I can't tell you. I can't tell anyone."

"You can tell me."

"Well . . ." Mimi sniffed and looked into his eyes. "No, I don't want to get you involved. You're too nice. I must be going."

"Mimi, wait—"

"Please, I must go."

"Let me fly you home before it starts to rain. I daresay I can go a bit faster. Come on, climb on my back. Where do you live?"

"In the Wildflower Woods under a May-apple."

Leon heard a deep, rasping cough coming from behind the rosemary hedge. "Shhh! Did you hear something?" he asked Mimi.

"Yes! No! I don't know!" she stammered, trembling with terror. "Help me, Leon. Please, take me home quickly!"

"Wait, wait. Let me take a look." Leon started toward the hedge.

"No, Leon! We must go *now*!"

The panic in Mimi's voice brought Leon back to her. She climbed on his back, and he took off swiftly, carrying her away from the Flowerpot District to the Wildflower Woods in the northeast corner of the Cottage Garden.

It was just starting to rain when they arrived at Mimi's little burrow under an umbrella-like May-apple plant. The burrow was made of mud and straw. It had a pebble terrace and a wooden door with a pine-needle doormat.

"Thank you for bringing me home," Mimi said, sounding somewhat calmer. "Would you like to come in for some tea and strawberry until the rain stops?"

"Sure, that would be nice."

As Mimi led Leon through the front door of her burrow, he thought he heard the mysterious cough again. And when he glanced back over his shoulder, he felt sure he saw something move behind a mound of dead leaves.

"Leon? Is something wrong?" asked Mimi.

"No, no, nothing. Nothing at all," he said, trying to sound nonchalant for he did not want to alarm her again.

TWO

"Please, have a seat," Mimi offered, and she guided Leon to a small twig chair. She lit a beeswax candle, then poured rainwater from a hickory barrel into a tiny stone kettle. Leon glanced about at the bare earthen floor, empty walls, and bed of straw.

"Forgive the look of my place," she said, putting the kettle on a beeswax burner. "But I only moved to the Garden a few days ago."

"I guess that's why I've never seen you before," said Leon. "My mother's noticed you, though. She saw you yesterday near the Lily Pond with a—a sort of odd-looking creature."

"Oh, that wasn't me!" said Mimi. She sounded upset again. "I was here all day yesterday."

"Hm, well, she must have been mistaken then," said Leon quickly. Anxious to change the subject, he looked around the room and caught sight of three dusty books lying on her bed. "My, don't these look interesting?" he said, flitting over to them.

"Oh! Those!" Before Leon could touch the books, Mimi darted to the bed and scooped them up. "They're nothing, really."

"Well, what—what are their titles?"

Mimi peered at the book spines. "Um—*Ants at War, Ants at Peace, Ants Forever*. Really, they're not very good."

"But they look so old. Are they rare?"

"Oh no, no, no. I just picked them up at a flea market. Ah-choo! Goodness, they're so dusty—let me move them out of our way."

Leon was puzzled as Mimi fluttered to the back of her burrow with the books. When she was out of sight, he quickly peeked out the window and studied her yard. He saw no signs of the coughing prowler.

"There," Mimi said, returning. She lifted her little kettle from the burner. Her hands seemed to be trembling as she poured the steamy rainwater into two buttercups filled with lemon grass.

Leon watched her, trying to figure out what was

troubling the beautiful butterfly. "Where'd you live before?" he asked.

"Far away . . . on an island," she said.

"Really? Where?"

"I think I'd rather not talk about it, if you don't mind," she said, looking at him sadly. "The past brings back some painful memories, Leon."

"Oh, of course." As Mimi cut two slices from a strawberry, Leon felt anger at the thought that anyone or anything would cause her pain. She seemed so nice.

She placed the tiny pieces of the fruit on the delicate petals of a sweet white violet, then served Leon. "Do you live alone?" she asked.

"No, I live with my mother—or 'La Mère,' as she calls herself these days."

"La Mère? It sounds French. Is she from France?"

"Far from it. She grew up in the Goatweed Patch next to Dogtick's place—a fact that she tries to hide."

"Really? Why?"

"I guess because she wants everyone in the snobby Flowerpot District to like her. She wants to be part of the 'in' crowd."

"Where's the Flowerpot District?"

"Where you dropped your scarf. We live between the Appleworms and the Salamanders. My mother'll do anything to be accepted by them. She's even given up flying and tries to walk, like the Salamanders. But she keeps falling again and again—sometimes hits her head."

"Oh, how sad."

"It is, rather."

"Leon, guess what falls down and never gets hurt."

"What?"

"Snow!"

As Leon chuckled, Mimi slapped her little knees and laughed a lovely, tinkling laugh. It touched Leon to see her happy for a moment. But then sorrow returned to her face. "You know, there was a time when I wanted to be accepted by everyone too," she said softly.

"Really?"

"Oh, yes. I prayed for yellow wings instead of blue. I never laughed because I didn't like my high little titter. I even—" She stopped.

"You what?" said Leon.

"I wore three pairs of dance tights so my legs wouldn't look so skinny."

"No kidding?" said Leon. "Me too. I mean I stopped wearing short-sleeved shirts because I thought my arms were too skinny."

"Oh, Leon, your arms are wonderful."

"Thank you," said Leon. He was amazed; he'd never had a conversation like this before.

"You know, some bad experiences have taught me that being yourself is the best thing in the world to be," said Mimi. "Only sometimes you're forced—" She shook her head as tears flooded her eyes.

"What's wrong, Mimi?" said Leon.

"Nothing." She smiled sadly, then began singing in her high little voice:

> *If you can't be yourself, friend,*
> *What's the point of living?*
> *If you can't be yourself, friend,*
> *You might as well give in.*

Leon could hardly speak. "Did you make that song up just now?" he asked with wonder.

She nodded.

"But that's the best song I ever heard."

"Oh." She smiled with embarrassment. "I guess you inspire me, Leon."

They held each other's gaze for a long moment. Then she whispered, "Would you like to see something very special?"

Leon nodded, enthralled.

"I really shouldn't show you this, but you won't tell anyone. Will you?"

"No, no."

"Good. I'll be right back. Close your eyes."

Leon did as he was told. His heart did soft, fluttery things as he inhaled the fresh scent of lemon tea and listened to the rain pattering on the thatched roof of the little burrow.

"You can open your eyes now," Mimi said, returning to him.

When Leon looked up, he was struck by a dazzling light coming from the top of her head. "Goodness," he breathed. "What's that?"

"Shhh. A diamond crown," she whispered. "Can you sing, Leon?"

"No, not really."

"Oh, I bet you sing beautifully. I can tell from your speaking voice. Please sing for me."

Leon laughed nervously. Then he cleared his throat and began crooning in a lovely bass:

> *Some enchanted evening,*
> *You may see a stranger,*
> *You may see a stranger*
> *Across a crowded room. . . .*

As he sang, Mimi began to dance.

With the tiny diamond crown sparkling on her head, she tiptoed gracefully around her burrow. Her blue iridescent wings fluttered up, then down, her cares and troubles seeming to fall away from her. She moved so perfectly in time with the melody that Leon felt as if they were both singing and both dancing. When she began to twirl around, he lifted his voice and sang as he'd never sung before:

> *And somehow you know,*
> *You know even then*
> *That somewhere you'll see her*
> *Again and again.*

THREE

Leon was bursting with happiness as he told his mother about the visit with Mimi. "And not only is she a great dancer, but she tells jokes and makes up songs. She invited me over on Saturday to help her build some shelves. She can't afford to spend any money on her place now—" He stopped to catch his breath.

La Mère was not impressed. She fanned herself

with a ginkgo leaf as she lay stretched out on her velvety cattail divan. "Don't be silly, dearie. She's not interested in you."

"What?"

"I told you yesterday I saw her hugging some horrible-looking bug. He was wearing a dirty red thing on his head and had an ugly patch over his eye."

"And I told you that you were wrong," said Leon, though not very confidently. "She said it wasn't her, and I believe her."

"Phooey, I've got good eyes, sonny. I know what I see. Furthermore, isn't she quite a bit older than you?"

"No—well, maybe just a little—but that doesn't matter."

"What kind of butterfly arrives penniless in town, Leon, and rents a burrow by herself in the Wildflower Woods? Whew!" La Mère fanned harder.

"*My* kind of butterfly!"

"Stop being silly. What will my friends think if they see you with her?"

"WHO CARES?"

"I care! She's a cheap little tramp!"

"How can you say that?" said Leon, hopping up and down with rage. "She's one of the nicest, kindest butterflies I've ever met. She's got troubles, and she needs friends—and you insult her! I hate you!"

"Leon, Leon, I just want something better for you. What about Muffy Salamander?"

"I hate Muffy Salamander! I hate all the snobs who live around here!" Leon shrieked. "I'm going to see Mimi on Saturday! And if you don't like it, I'll move out."

"Well, I don't like it," said La Mère.

"Fine. Good. Then I'm leaving." And having said that, Leon soared out of La Mère's cracked geranium pot, without even a glance back.

Leon left the Flowerpot District and flew swiftly to the middle of the Cottage Garden. There, near the stone birdbath, was the snug little home of his best friends, Rosie and Little Pickles. The two ladybugs lived in a tiny cottage under a moonflower vine.

Though a bit slow and clumsy on the wing, Rosie and Little Pickles had wonderful, energetic personalities. They earned their living making tulip cradles for the Garden babies and catering picnics and parties.

When Leon peeked in their kitchen window, he caught them wearing their matching polka-dotted dresses with pink aprons. Though the birchwood walls and floor were scrubbed bone white, the kitchen was in its usual disarray. Tiny copper saucepans, soup pots, and muffin tins were stacked everywhere. Bouquets of dried thyme, mint, and basil hung from the low ceiling. Jars filled with pickles, sauces, and relishes crowded the countertops.

At the moment, the two ladybugs were making pies. As Rosie pressed some dough down into one of five acorn caps, she called to Little Pickles, "Don't forget the cinnamon!"

"I won't," said Little Pickles, sprinkling the brown powder over peach slices and blueberries in a walnut mixing bowl.

"Oh, and don't forget the nutmeg—" said Rosie.

"Hi!" said Leon, poking his head through their window.

The two ladybugs screamed.

"Gracious!" said Little Pickles, shaking her spoon

at him. "I'm going to beat you with this!"

"I'll throw dough in your face next time you scare us like that, Leafy!" said Rosie, calling Leon by his nickname. Rosie nicknamed everyone. Long ago she'd started calling her friend Bess "Little Pickles" because Bess made the best pickles in the Garden.

"Just in time. We're making blueberry-peach pie!" Little Pickles said.

"Oh, great," said Leon without enthusiasm.

"All righty, let's spoon that in here now," said Rosie to Little Pickles. Together, they piled the filling into the five pie shells, then drizzled lemon juice and butter over it.

Little Pickles slipped the acorn pie plates into a clay oven as Rosie licked the spoon.

"Mmm, mmm!" Rosie said, her eyes wide. "Here, Leafy, *you* can lick the bowl."

"No thanks. I'm not very hungry."

"*What?* Not lick the bowl! Little Pickles, he must be sick."

Before Leon could say another word, Rosie and Little Pickles yanked off their aprons. They grabbed Leon and led him into their sun-dappled sitting room.

They pushed him onto a feather-stuffed cornhusk sofa, then plopped down beside him.

"Now," said Rosie. "What's wrong?"

Leon sighed. "I have a new friend named Mimi, but my mother doesn't like her, and we just had a terrible fight, and now I don't have any place to live, and—"

"Whoa, whoa," said Rosie. "One thing at a time. First, you can live here with us."

"Of course," said Little Pickles.

Leon smiled, touched by their kindness.

"Second—tell us *all* about this Mimi."

As the three friends sat close to one another in the warm afternoon light, Leon told the ladybugs about meeting the gossamer-winged butterfly. He told them how Mimi seemed sad and frightened. He told them about the strange cough behind the hedge. He told them all about her burrow, her snow joke, and her odd and wonderful little song. He almost told them about the secret diamond crown, but he stopped himself just in time. He did mention, however, that Mimi danced like a diamond sparkling in the dawn.

When he finished, Rosie and Little Pickles just stared at him. "Gracious," said Little Pickles.

"His first girlfriend," whispered Rosie.

"*Girlfriend?* She's not my *girlfriend*," said Leon. "I don't even know her, and she's older than me. She's not a *girlfriend*. She's just a friend."

"Sure," said Rosie. She stared wistfully into the distance and imitated Leon— "And she dances like a diamond sparkling in the dawn."

"Cut it out," said Leon. "She's new in town, that's all. I'm trying to be a good citizen and make her feel welcome."

"Leon! Leon!" came a voice from outside.

"Wha-at the—" Leon fluttered to the door.

"Come here, you brat! You can't just move out like that!" Using a leaf-stem cane, La Mère was hobbling down a molehill toward the cottage.

"Leafy, look! Your mom's walking," said Rosie, peering out the window.

"She's pathetic," said Leon. "She's trying to walk like the Salamanders." He charged outside. "Mother, what in the world are you doing here?"

"I want you to come home! Now!" said La Mère.

"Forget it. I'm staying here until you accept Mimi into our lives."

"Accept Mimi into our lives!" La Mère waved her walking cane. "This is not an opera, Leon! This is real life. You can't just go around making friends with the first tacky oddball who comes along."

"Tacky oddball?? That's disgusting!" said Leon. "You can't talk about Mimi that way."

"I can, dearie, because I have your own best interests at heart. And if you don't come home now, I'll have to take action."

"What sort of action, ma'am?" called Rosie.

"Horrible action, dearie!" said La Mère, pointing her cane at Rosie. "Horrible, horrible, horrible action."

"Well, take action!" said Leon. "Take it right home with you!"

"You'll be sorry," said La Mère. "Remember, you only get one mother in this world!" With that, she turned and started hobbling back the way she'd come.

"Why don't you fly, Mother?" Leon shouted after her. "Butterflies are supposed to fly!"

"NO! They're supposed to mind their mothers!" And with that, La Mère disappeared over the crest of the molehill.

"Mimi's my girlfriend, Mother!" shouted Leon. "Get that? *My girlfriend!*"

"Gracious," said Little Pickles as Leon collapsed on the cornhusk sofa.

"We didn't know you had it in you, *dearie*," said Rosie.

FOUR

All Leon could think about that week was Mimi. Mimi, Mimi, Mimi. Finally on Saturday, in the early morning mist, he collected a tiny bouquet of silver thyme. Little Pickles gave him a jar of watermelon pickle, and Rosie tied a tiny peach-colored ascot around his neck. Then Leon waved good-bye to his two best friends and took off for Mimi's burrow in the Wildflower Woods.

He felt light with joy as he sailed over the hazy Cottage Garden—over the stone birdbath, over the

Lily Pond, the old sundial, and the meadow rue. But as he fluttered close to the Wildflower Woods, he realized he was quite early. Mimi wasn't expecting him until noon. So he lit down under a lilac bush to rest for a while.

Leon plucked a purple flower and put it in the buttonhole of his jacket. He straightened his little ascot. Sitting peacefully in the fragrant shade, he began dreaming about his future with Mimi for the hundredth time that week. Perhaps one day they'd marry in Bee City, where the most beautiful weddings took place. Perhaps he'd even sing their song at the wedding. He took a deep breath, then began in his gentle bass:

> *Some enchanted evening,*
> *When you find your true love,*
> *When you feel her call you*
> *Across a crowded room,*
> *Then fly to her side, —*

But his song was interrupted by loud, ugly laughter. "Dumb enchanted cheese dog," sang a mocking voice.

When Leon whirled around, he saw Walter Dogtick standing nearby in the bristle grass, clutching a big sack.

"Hello, Leon, little son of *La Mère*," Walter said sarcastically. "How 'bout this for a love song:"

> *Dogtick, Leafywing, Dogtick, Leafywing,*
> *Why can't a Dogtick dance with a Leafywing?*

As the old tick sang, he danced a clumsy little dance. Leon felt sorry for him. Walter Dogtick had been hurt and angry ever since Pupa Leafwing had changed her name to "La Mère" and moved from the Goatweed Patch to the Flowerpot District. Though they'd been best friends when they were young, La Mère now refused to recognize Dogtick in public.

"How's that for a real love song?" said Walter.

"Fine, Wally."

"You know, Leon, I knew your mother when she was just a fat little caterpillar."

"I know, Wally."

The old tick chuckled and tugged on his dirty old sack. "Well, I got something that will get her back now," he said.

Leon saw a tiny piece of purple cloth sticking out of the opening of the sack. "What's in there?" he asked Dogtick.

"Wouldn't you like to know?" Walter said.

"Okay. Look, I'm not bothering you, Wally," said Leon. "So why don't you just move along?"

Walter Dogtick laughed loudly. Then, dragging his

soiled sack behind him, he crept off, singing:

> *Dogtick, Leafywing, Dogtick, Leafywing,*
> *Why can't a Dogtick dance with a Leafywing?*

As the crude voice faded away, Leon shuddered. The lonely Dogtick depressed him. He fluffed up his ascot, picked up the thyme bouquet and watermelon pickle, then fluttered into the air.

As soon as Leon soared above the wild strawberries and pink pasture roses, his good spirits returned. Gliding toward Mimi's burrow, he pictured them someday living in a little burrow of their own. Perhaps it would be carpeted with corn silk. A tuft of lavender would be their bed. Their home would always be warm and cozy and filled with the scent of lemon tea.

He was smiling as he landed near the May-apple.

It was a long moment before he realized something terrible had happened. At first, he simply stared at the caved-in burrow: the ugly mounds of dirt littered across the ground, the scattered straw, pebbles, and pine needles.

"Mimi?" he called in a frightened voice.

Horror filled him as he stared at the torn pages of her books, and her twig chairs broken in half.

Then he heard someone cough behind the bushes. "Who's there?" He darted to the brush. The grass rustled, but there was no sign of anyone.

Dazed, Leon rushed back to the wreckage. He threw aside the twigs and straw, expecting to find his friend among the ruins. But all he found were her little dark glasses.

"MIMI!" he screamed.

FIVE

The fragrance of night-blooming moon-flower filled Rosie and Little Pickles's kitchen. And as a cool breeze blew through their window, the cream-colored curtains rose and fell like ghosts.

"Calm down, Leafy," said Rosie when Leon had finished his terrible story. "I'm sure she's still alive."

"How can you be sure?" Leon cried. Wearing

Mimi's dark glasses, he was fluttering frantically about the kitchen.

"For one thing, you'd have found her body among the wreckage if she'd been killed."

"That's right." Little Pickles nodded.

"Then where is she?" said Leon. "What happened to her? I flew everywhere looking for her. I asked at the Lily Pond, the Flowerpots, the stone wall— everywhere!"

"Did you consider that she might have been kidnapped?" said Rosie.

"Kidnapped?"

"Yes."

Leon stopped fluttering. "No, I didn't think of that. Wait a minute, wait a minute." He sat and stared at Rosie. "She *was* kidnapped. Yes, she was! And I know exactly who did it."

"Who?" said Rosie and Little Pickles.

"Walter Dogtick," said Leon. "I saw Walter Dogtick coming from the Wildflower Woods just before I got to Mimi's. He was carrying a sack. A big one—big enough to hold Mimi! And I saw something purple sticking out of it. Mimi's scarf!" Leon nearly choked with excitement. "It was her scarf! She was . . ."

"Oh, Leafy, *stop it,*" said Rosie. "Dogtick always carries that dirty old sack. He's a scavenger. He likes to collect junk. You know that."

"No, no! This is too much of a coincidence! That's it! That's it!" Leon pounded the table, knocking over sauce bottles and pie plates.

"Honey, stop," said Rosie. "Get ahold of yourself. And take off those ridiculous sunglasses."

Leon heaved a great sigh. He took off Mimi's dark glasses, revealing his red, teary eyes. "Then where is she?" he asked in a small voice. "I looked every-where."

"We know you did, sweetie," said Little Pickles.

"Look, before you fly off and accuse anyone, maybe we should try to get some help," said Rosie.

"Who can help us?" said Leon.

"I don't know."

"Wait," said Little Pickles in a low, whispery voice. "I have an idea."

"What?"

"Maybe we should go see Spider Kane, Rosie."

A smile slowly crossed Rosie's face. "Of *course*. Why didn't I think of that?"

"Who's Spider Kane?" said Leon.

"He's amazing, Leon," said Little Pickles. "I've never met him, but Rosie's told me all about him."

"Spider Kane's an old friend of mine. I served with him in the Mosquito Wars," said Rosie.

"He was wounded in battle," said Little Pickles excitedly. "Two of his legs are crippled, but he still gets around quite remarkably. He travels all over the world!"

"Not only does he travel, he's also a fine jazz musician," said Rosie.

"He plays the clarinet!" said Little Pickles.

"Yes, and he composes music, and he writes and directs plays in his spare time."

"Well, a traveling jazz musician playwright is not what we need now," said Leon.

"Oh, but he's also a brilliant detective!" said Little Pickles.

"Is he ever!" said Rosie.

"Really?" said Leon. "Then why haven't I ever heard of him?"

"Since he moved into the Cottage Garden last autumn, Spy's been—that's my nickname for him, it's short for Spider—anyway, he's been . . ."

"A bit of a hermit, right, Rosie?" said Little Pickles.

"Oh yes, that's a good way to put it."

"He mentioned he was writing a new play or something, didn't he, Rosie?" said Little Pickles.

"I thought you said you'd never met him," Leon said to Little Pickles.

"She hasn't," said Rosie quickly. "I told her all these things. Yes, Spy's been very busy and reclusive."

"Well, let's not disturb him then," said Leon.

"Oh no, no, no. I think we should disturb him," said Little Pickles.

"Of course we should!" said Rosie. "Spy loves a mystery. How about it, Leon?"

"Well, okay. But I don't know—"

"Don't worry," said Rosie. "I promise you that whatever happens, you won't be sorry. I'm sure you've never met anyone like Spider Kane in your whole life."

As Leon flew through the windy dark with Rosie and Little Pickles clinging to his back, strange sounds filled his ears. It was as if the wind rustling through the grass were gossiping about the evil that had happened under the May-apple.

> *She's gone, gone, never see her again,*
> *Never, never, never, never, never . . .*

"No!" cried Leon. But his voice could not be heard above the mad whisperings of the night.

Part II

SIX

"I think I've found it! I hear music!" Rosie shouted as she led the way along the crumbling stone wall, searching for the entrance to Spider Kane's home.

Leon and Little Pickles followed her into a tiny, cavelike hollow between two stones. Then they groped their way down a dark tunnel that led to the elegant chambers of Spider Kane.

They found him playing a jazz tune on a clarinet made from a hollow river reed. The lively music moved

in time with a leaping candle flame, and shadows danced on the chalky stone walls and silken floor. Beside the spider was a briarwood pipe and a golden goblet made from a touch-me-not flower. Around his shoulders was a paisley dressing gown.

When the jazzy song ended, Rosie spoke softly: "Spy?"

Spider Kane jerked around to face his three visitors. Then he burst into laughter. "Lieutenant Rose! Good heavens!"

The two hugged each other warmly. Then Rosie said, "Spy, I'd like you to meet two dear friends,

Little Pickles and Leon Leafwing—"

"Hello, Miss Pickles! What a pleasure," said Spider Kane in his deep, velvety voice.

"Gracious," said Little Pickles, trembling with excitement.

As Spider Kane turned to him, Leon quickly slipped on Mimi's dark glasses to hide his teary, swollen eyes.

"Hello, Mr. Leafwing, very pleased to meet you, too," said Spider Kane.

"Thank you. You can call me Leon."

"Fine, Leon. Now sit! All of you, sit and let me get you something to drink!" Spider Kane moved across the room with a slight limp. Then he poured a dark red liquid into three golden touch-me-not goblets. "Vintage cherry juice," he said. "How about some dinner? Parsnip pie? Peas in patty shells?"

"No thank you, Mr. Kane," said Little Pickles. "We've already eaten."

"Ah yes, I see that now. You dined on black bean soup."

"How did you know?" stammered Little Pickles.

"I've studied food stains for many years, Miss

Pickles," he said. "The dark blotches on your blouse are definitely black bean soup."

"Oh dear," said Little Pickles, blushing and putting her hand over the stains.

Rosie laughed. "I see you haven't lost your touch, Spy."

"No indeed, Lieutenant Rose."

"Good," said Rosie. "Because we need your help tonight. Leon is in great distress."

"Ahh." The spider fixed his eyes on the butterfly. "Would you kindly remove your glasses, sir?"

When Leon took off Mimi's dark glasses, Spider Kane stared at his red eyes. "Your girlfriend," the spider said softly.

"How did you know?"

"Your tear-stained face speaks a thousand words, Leon. As does the wilted lilac in your buttonhole. I assume you paid a call on her—and she wasn't there?"

"That's right," said Leon sadly. "Her books were torn apart, her furniture was broken. I just found these little glasses—"

"Ah, let me see." Spider Kane took the dark glasses from Leon and studied them. "But the gossamer-winged lady was missing," he said quietly.

Leon gasped. "How—how did you know she was a gossamer-winged butterfly?"

"I have the rare gift of being able to make instant and perfect calculations of size without the use of a measuring tool," said Spider Kane. "I can tell you that these dark glasses exactly fit the head of a gossamer-winged butterfly."

"You know the head size of a butterfly?"

"I know the head sizes of over two hundred different kinds of butterflies, my friend. If these belonged to one of your own species, they'd be half a micrometer larger."

As Leon laughed with astonishment, Spider Kane smiled and lit his pipe.

SEVEN

Spider Kane was silent when Leon finished the story of how he'd met Mimi. He puffed on his pipe and stared at the flickering candle flame, deep in thought. "So," he said finally, "the sky was over-

cast when she dropped the silk scarf near the Appleworms' pot?"

"Yes, that's right."

"Yet she was wearing dark glasses?"

"Well, yes . . ."

"And you thought you heard someone cough behind a bush?"

"Yes, and I felt as if we were being watched. I
heard the same coughing noise outside her home."

"Hm. And you say that she seemed quite anxious?
As if she were afraid that someone might be following her?"

"Yes," said Leon.

Spider Kane nodded, then took a sip from his
golden goblet. "Did you see any items of interest in
her burrow? Anything someone might want to steal?"

"Well . . . she'd just moved in, and she didn't have
many things. She seemed quite penniless, in fact."

"So there was nothing there?"

"Just some old books from a flea market."

"What kind of books?"

"Um—it was a trilogy of ant novels."

"*Yes?*" Spider Kane leaned forward, his eyes burning with interest. "Are you certain, Leon?"

"Yes. Why?"

"Nothing." The spider bit his thin lip and settled back in his chair. He relit his pipe and puffed hard. "Go on. What else? What else did you see?"

"Nothing, really."

"You're not telling the truth, Leon."

"I'm not?"

"No. When butterflies lie, they often glance to the left, as you just did."

"Oh." Leon shifted uncomfortably. He hated breaking Mimi's confidence.

"Yes?" said Spider Kane. "What are you concealing?"

"Well," Leon took a deep breath. "She did have a tiny little crown in her possession."

"Crown? What kind of crown?"

"Um—a diamond crown."

"Good heavens!" The spider jerked forward. "Did it not strike you as odd that a penniless butterfly would have a diamond crown?"

"Well, yes, it did, but . . ."

"But? But?"

"Well, I . . . um . . . she danced and I sang . . . and it . . ." Leon swallowed, overcome with embarrassment. "It didn't occur to me to ask . . ." He stopped. It was impossible to explain that magic moment with Mimi wearing her crown.

"I see," said Spider Kane softly.

An awkward silence filled the room.

"Well!" said Spider Kane. "What else can you tell me, son?"

"Uh . . . well . . . I know Rosie thinks I'm wrong about this, but . . ."

"Yes?" said Spider Kane.

"I don't want to point the blame at anyone, but . . ."

"Yes? Yes?"

"I did see Walter Dogtick coming from the Wildflower Woods a moment before I got to Mimi's. He was dragging along a sack. And I saw a tiny piece of purple cloth sticking out of it."

"Yes? So?"

"Well, Mimi had a purple scarf, see. So I wondered if maybe she could—well, might possibly have been inside that sack."

"Good heavens, I hope not," said Spider Kane. He pulled off his paisley dressing gown and grabbed his gray wool cloak. "It's time I visited the scene of the crime," he said. "Get your hats, my friends!"

Since none of them wore hats, their departure was immediate.

EIGHT

The Wildflower Woods sparkled with dewdrops. In the pale light of dawn, Spider Kane, Leon, Rosie, and Little Pickles stared at the wreckage under the May-apple. Though he hadn't slept all night, Leon felt very alert as he waited for Spider Kane's conclusions.

At first the spider was silent, only nodding to himself. Then suddenly he was limping about everywhere—touching this, examining that, missing nothing. "Aha!" he shouted, crouching and digging in the dirt.

"What?" cried Leon.

"Aha!" he shouted again.

"Gracious, what is it, Mr. Kane?" said Little Pickles.

"Ahhh." The spider came to a halt and stared at the ground. After a long pause he rose from his crouching position and lit his pipe. "There was much fighting and struggle," he said. "I see wing tracks everywhere. Also—the diamond crown you mentioned, Leon, is nowhere to be found."

"Oh, that's right," said Leon. He fluttered above the wreckage again. "And I don't see Mimi's silk scarf, either. Only the books are still here. But oh—look at this!"

The others hurried over.

"There're only two books!" he said, pointing to the torn pages of the Ant Trilogy, lying on the ground, flipping in the breeze. "See—*Ants at Peace* and *Ants Forever*. There was another one, a third book! Where is it?"

"Good question." Spider Kane stroked his chin and began combing through the wreckage again.

"He's right, Spy," said Rosie. "There're only two books."

"What can that mean, Mr. Kane?" said Little Pickles.

Spider Kane didn't answer. He was gaping at the dirt floor beneath the May-apple. "Good heavens," he said under his breath. Then he crouched down and gingerly touched the ground. As the others rushed to see what he was doing, he shouted, "Stop! Stop! Or you'll destroy the remaining letters."

"What letters?" said Rosie.

"There's a message scratched into the dirt here," he said.

"What does it say?" cried Leon.

"See for yourself. Unfortunately much of it has been wiped out, perhaps in the struggle between Mimi and her assailant."

As Leon fluttered close to the ground, he read:

HE   R MOTH ENDS THE D

"What does it mean?" he cried.

But suddenly he heard a cough coming from the woods. Before Leon could speak, Spider Kane rushed toward the brush. "Halt!" he shouted. Leon's heart pounded as the spider shouted, "Come out! Show yourself!"

Spider Kane rustled about the brush for a moment. Then there was silence.

"Spy?" called Rosie.

The grass moved again. Then Spider Kane appeared. As he limped slowly back toward the others, there was a look of amazement on his face. "I don't believe it," he said to himself.

"What, Spy?" said Rosie. "Did you see someone?"

"No, Rosie, I didn't see a soul. But I did hear a cough," he said with an odd smile.

Spider Kane rummaged in the pocket of his cloak and pulled out a piece of paper. He placed the paper over the letters scratched under the May-apple and carefully traced them. Then after studying the message, he whispered, "Ah, now I understand."

"Understand what?" said Leon. "What, Mr. Kane?"

It was a long moment before Spider Kane looked up from the paper. And when he did, his face was filled with dismay. "Everything. Everything, Leon," he said quietly. "I'm afraid, my friend, we have a disaster on our hands."

Spider Kane crumpled the paper and tossed it onto the ground. Then he wrapped his gray cloak around

him and said, "I've been a fool. I must leave you now."

"Where're you going?" cried Leon.

"I'm going to visit a very old comrade."

"Who? Why? What's going on?" said Leon.

"I will explain everything later, Leon. Right now, go home with Rosie and Little Pickles."

"Tell us now!" said Leon.

"No, no," said Spider Kane. "Not until I hold cold facts in my hands, rather than mere suspicions." And with that, he turned and limped away.

NINE

"This will cheer us up," said Little Pickles, as she pulled a tray of sweet potato scones from her clay oven.

"Not me. I can't eat," said Leon. "My stomach's too nervous." He chewed the end of his pencil as he hovered over the paper on which Spider Kane had copied the mysterious message:

HE   R MOTH ENDS THE D

"Let's see," he muttered. "The only word we can read is MOTH. But what does that mean? MOTH." He stared at Little Pickles as she served the scones with cherry jam. "What moth? Do you know any moths?"

"Lucinda Moth taught me in first grade," said Little Pickles. "How about scones with pumpkin butter?"

"No thanks."

"Leafy, let's give this up for now," pleaded Rosie. "Wait till Spy gets back."

"Wait? I can't wait. Every minute's important. Let me see . . . I still think HE might be part of the word *help*."

"But so many words begin with HE," said Little Pickles. "*Heart, heck, heehaw—*"

"No, I think Mimi must have written *help* when she realized she was about to be attacked," said Leon. "And D—I have my suspicions about D."

"Oh, tons of words start with D, Leafy," said Rosie.

"*Doughnut, dumplings, doodad,*" said Little Pickles.

"No, no, none of them. It's *Dogtick*," growled Leon.

"Oh, c'mon, Leafy, let's not start that again," said Rosie.

"Why not?" said Leon. "Just consider it for a moment. ENDS—that probably just means *ends*. Wait a minute, wait a minute. If we try the word *help* and *Dogtick*, what do we have?" He scribbled beneath the letters:

HELP!   RMOTH ENDS THE DOGTICK

"Ah! Look!" he said, holding up the paper.

"That doesn't make a bit of sense," said Rosie. "Why

don't we try leaving Dogtick out of it?"

"Wait, wait, wait," Leon said. He closed his eyes and mouthed slowly, "*Mo-th, mo-th-er, mother!* Oh wow." Beneath his scribbles, he added another line. "Now what if ENDS were *sends*?" he muttered. He added another line. "And R were part of *your*?" He scribbled yet another line.

When he was through, he let out a yelp and thrust the paper at Rosie and Little Pickles. They read:

```
HE          R MOTH ENDS THE D
HELP!       R MOTH ENDS THE DOGTICK
HELP!       R MOTHER ENDS THE DOGTICK
HELP!       R MOTHER SENDS THE DOGTICK
HELP!   YOUR MOTHER SENDS THE DOGTICK
```

"That's it! That's it! *Help! Your mother sends the Dogtick!*" Leon shouted. He jumped up and down, beating his wings wildly.

"Oh, you're wrong," said Rosie.

"I'm right!" shouted Leon. "My mother swore to take action! Horrible action! She got Dogtick to do

her dirty work for her. That explains everything!"
His wings began to hammer the air.

"Wait, wait, wait, Leafy. Wait for Spy—"

"No! I'll kill her! I'll kill her!" said Leon, and he
zoomed out of the cottage and headed straight toward
the Flowerpot District.

TEN

La Mère Leafwing's cracked flowerpot was
abuzz with chatter as the Women's Bug Club ate their
lunch around a water lily table.

"La Mère, your *soupe à la tomate* is so delightful,"
said Lou Salamander. "I'm ever so pleased you're a
member of our club now."

"Thank you, Lou," said La Mère, glowing.

"La Mère, darling, what a beautiful dandelion wig,"
said Midge Appleworm. "It's just like mine—though
not quite as fluffy."

"Oh, thank you, darling, but yours is the very best,
of course," said La Mère. "I wish mine were only
half so elegant."

"What a fascinating-looking book," said Nymph Latell, pointing to the dusty volume on La Mère's cattail divan.

"Oh, that," said La Mère. "Yes, a friend gave it to me as a gift. Along with some good news that cheered me right up."

"Ooo! What? Tell!" said the others.

"Well, as some of you may know, my son and I had a little quarrel the other day."

"Oh, yes. The gossip I've heard is that he's be-

59

come infatuated with a fluttery blue creature," said Midge Appleworm, batting her eyes cattily.

"Well, that's all over now," said La Mère. "That little fly-by-night has danced right out of town. I'm certain *mon fils* will be returning to his senses very soon. So, change those rumors, will you, dearies?" She laughed happily.

"Ooo la la! Where did you get that?" said Nymph Latell, pointing to a scarf hanging on La Mère's pine cone hatrack.

La Mère fluttered to the hatrack and draped the purple silk scarf around her neck. "My friend with the book gave me this also. *Très belle*, no?"

"Wait a *minute*!" said Midge Appleworm. The plump worm rose from the table and lunged for La Mère. "That is *my* silk scarf from China! Stolen from me three weeks ago! Thief! Thief!"

Before La Mère could answer, Leon burst into the flowerpot. "You witch! You witch!" he shouted. "Why did you do it?"

"What?" screamed La Mère hysterically. "Do what? What?"

"Kidnap her!" he shrieked.

"And steal from me!" yelled Midge. She pointed at the book on the cattail divan. "And I'll bet you stole that, too!"

When Leon looked at the old book, he felt faint. "*Ants at War.* Oh, Mother, how could you?" he asked in a strangled voice.

"WHAT?" screamed La Mère.

"Order Dogtick to kidnap her and then steal her things."

"Kidnap who? I didn't, I didn't! I'm no kidnapper! I'm no thief!"

"Then how did you get this?" said Midge Appleworm, wapping La Mère with the purple scarf.

"I didn't steal it," sobbed La Mère. "It was a gift!"

But Midge Appleworm grabbed her pea-pod pocketbook and started for the door. "Tell it to the judge, Pupa," she said. "Come, ladies."

With that, the three members of the Women's Bug Club huffed out of La Mère's cracked geranium pot. "*Au revoir,* thief!" Nymph Latell called over her shoulder.

"I don't understand!" La Mère cried. "I don't understand any of this."

"Mother," said Leon coldly. "Just tell me. Where is she?"

"I don't know what you're talking about, Leon! I'm innocent! I'm innocent of everything!"

"You're lying!" he shouted. "WHERE IS SHE?"

"Excuse me for interrupting, Leon," said a deep, velvety voice. "But I do believe your mother is telling the truth."

And with that, Spider Kane crawled into the cracked clay pot, with Rosie and Little Pickles right behind.

ELEVEN

"Who . . . who are you?" sobbed La Mère.

"My name is Spider Kane, ma'am. Sit and calm yourself."

"My mother did it, Mr. Kane. I have proof now," said Leon.

"I DIDN'T DO ANYTHING, YOU IDIOT!"

"There, there," said Spider Kane. "Calm down, everyone."

"Perhaps you're not aware, Mr. Kane, my mother has *this* in her possession," said Leon. "And *this*." He held up Mimi's scarf and book. "See? Proof she's guilty."

"I'm not guilty! Those were gifts from a friend."

"Indeed they were," said Spider Kane. "Gifts from one who cares for you—and wishes you would be his friend again, no?"

"How did you know Walter Dogtick gave me those things?" asked La Mère, stunned.

"I had no difficulty recognizing the tick tracks around Mimi's residence," said Spider Kane. "But I can assure you—all of you—that Walter Dogtick did not harm the butterfly. And technically he did not steal from her, either. The poor fellow arrived on the scene after she'd disappeared and took only what he thought she'd left behind to be discarded."

"But Mr. Kane," said Leon. "I figured out what the message under the May-apple says—*Help! Your mother sends the Dogtick.* Mimi must have scratched it in the dirt when she realized Dogtick was about to break into her home."

Spider Kane smiled. "Good work, son. But I'm afraid you're completely wrong. The message means something else entirely."

"Really? What, Spy?" said Rosie.

"I'll share my conclusions this evening at eight o'clock. You are all invited to my home." Spider Kane wrapped his cloak around him and prepared to leave. "Oh—" he said, turning to La Mère. "I shall also invite Walter Dogtick, ma'am. And Colonel and Mrs. Appleworm. We'll prove your innocence, once and for all. *Oui?*"

"*Merci*, Mr. Kane," La Mère said tearfully. "*Merci.*"

TWELVE

As the guests arrived at the elegant chambers of Spider Kane, they found him seated before a pale green leaf screen, playing his clarinet. Beside him was a mushroom table on which sat the copy of *Ants at War* and the purple silk scarf. Bean-pod chairs were placed in a semicircle with name cards on them.

As Spider Kane's soulful blues tune echoed through his stone chambers, the guests stumbled about, locating their seats. "What is this? Symphony Hall?" grumbled Colonel Appleworm, lowering his rotund body onto a bean pod.

"Hush," said Midge Appleworm.

Only when Spider Kane had concluded his mournful song did he look at the group. "Good evening," he said slowly. Then in the soft, flickering candlelight his gaze traveled from Leon to Rosie, to Little Pickles, to Colonel Appleworm, to Midge Appleworm, to La Mère, and finally to Walter Dogtick.

"Thank you all for coming," he said. "Let's begin." He put down his clarinet, then picked up the purple scarf from the exhibit table. "First, the mystery of the silk scarf. When did your scarf disappear, Mrs. Appleworm?"

"It was stolen three weeks ago while we were sleeping one night. It's a very expensive piece of silk made by the Wang Worms of China."

"A very expensive piece of silk made by the Wang

Worms of China," said Dogtick mockingly.

La Mère snickered.

"Now see here!" said Colonel Appleworm, turning to Dogtick.

"Come, come, let's act like grownups," said Spider Kane. "Mrs. Appleworm, was the burglar who broke into your flowerpot ever caught?"

"Not until now." Midge glared at La Mère.

"Oh, go blow your nose," said La Mère.

Dogtick laughed loudly and winked at La Mère. Leon was surprised to see his mother wink back.

"Thank you, Mrs. Appleworm," said Spider Kane. "'We'll let the mystery of the scarf rest for the time being. Now I'd like to introduce our first guest of the evening. Doctor Ant?"

From behind the leaf screen stepped the largest black carpenter ant Leon had ever seen. The enormous ant wore a stocking cap, a huge overcoat, and Italian lace-up shoes. On his back was a large hump.

"Allow me to introduce Dr. T. K. Ant, head librarian of the National Ant Archives," said Spider

Kane. "Dr. Ant recently sought my services for another investigation. Doctor, could you please describe the incident that occurred at the Ant Archives one month before the Appleworm robbery?"

The ant cleared his throat, then spoke in a tiny falsetto. "One night, while the workers at the National Ant Archives slept, our rare-book room was robbed of three priceless manuscripts."

Spider Kane picked up Mimi's copy of *Ants at War* from the exhibit table. "Is this one of your missing manuscripts, Doctor?"

"'Indeed it is."

Leon groaned. But Spider Kane did not look at him. "Thank you, Doctor."

Dr. Ant took a little bow and went back behind the screen.

"Now I'd like to introduce a bee who recently sought my services," said Spider Kane. "General?"

No one appeared.

"General?" said Spider Kane.

"Be right there," someone hummed.

A moment later, from behind the leaf screen stepped

a portly bumblebee shrouded in a bright blue cape with a blue soldier cap pulled down around his ears. Leon noticed that oddly enough the bee was also wearing Italian lace-up shoes—just like the ones worn by Dr. T. K. Ant.

"Who's this clown?" mumbled Colonel Appleworm.

"Hush," said Midge as she and the others leaned forward, spellbound.

"I'd like to introduce Major General Robert Bum, steward of the queen and deputy treasurer of Bee City," said Spider Kane. "Bob, did a burglary also occur this spring in Bee City? A robbery of the worst kind?"

"Mmm-hmm," said Major General Bum.

"The Queen Bee's diamond crown was stolen. Correct?" said Spider Kane.

"Mmm-hmm."

Leon groaned again and covered his face.

"A crown matching the description I gave you of the one Leon saw at Mimi's?" said Spider Kane.

"Mmm-hmm. Mmm-hmm." Major General Bum dropped his head and hummed sorrowfully. "Hmmmmmmmmmmmmmmmmmmmmmmmmm."

"Thank you, Bob," said Spider Kane.

"Hmmmmmmmmmmmmmmmmmmmmmmmmmmmmmm-mmmmmmmmmmmmmm."

"Thank you, Bob!"

Major General Bum shook himself, then buzzed back behind the leaf screen.

The group broke into excited murmuring.

"Gracious," said Little Pickles. "I think I'm beginning to see the light."

"Yes," said Spider Kane. "I imagine all of you are groping toward the same conclusion."

"No, no," Leon moaned.

"*She* stole all those things, didn't she, Mr. Kane?" shouted La Mère triumphantly. "That tacky Mimi! What did I tell you, Leon—your friend was a desperate thief."

"Indeed, Mimi was desperate, ma'am," said Spider Kane. "Not many of us would risk our lives to mend the mischief done by others."

"What do you mean, Spy?" said Rosie.

"Mimi was not a thief. She was only trying to *return* the stolen items to their rightful owners."

"Oh, whadya mean?" said Dogtick.

"If you had not trampled the message scratched in the dirt under the May-apple, Mr. Dogtick, we might have spared you and Mrs. Leafwing a great deal of embarrassment."

Spider Kane tacked a large piece of paper to his leaf screen and wrote:

HE   R MOTH ENDS THE D

"I'm afraid this does not mean *Help! Your mother sends the Dogtick,* Leon. If you study it a bit more, you'll see there's not enough room between MOTH and *ENDS* to add *E, R,* and *S.*"

"Oh, you're right. I'm an idiot," said Leon.

"It was a good try, my friend. And I wish for Mimi's sake you'd been right. For the real message, I'm afraid, is utterly horrifying."

Spider Kane turned back to the paper and slowly filled in the missing letters. When he stepped aside, the group read:

THE EMPEROR MOTH ENDS THE DAY

"The message under the May-apple was not a cry

72

for help from Mimi," Spider Kane said softly. "It was the arrogant boasting of an insane moth."

THIRTEEN

As Spider Kane lit his pipe, murmurs of confusion rippled through the crowd.

"What do you mean, Mr. Kane?" cried Leon.

"The Emperor Moth has kidnapped Mimi," said Spider Kane.

"But who is he? Who's the Emperor Moth?"

"Allow me to introduce one who can answer that far better than I." Spider Kane stepped behind the leaf screen and a moment later ushered out one of the strangest-looking moths Leon had ever seen.

Oddly enough, the moth wore the same Italian lace-up shoes as Dr. Ant and General Bum. But the rest of his clothing was considerably shabbier. He had a soiled red bandanna tied around his head and a black patch over one eye. His other eye twitched as a creepy smile cracked his face.

But suddenly a deep, racking cough wiped the smile

away. It was the same cough Leon had heard behind the rosemary hedge and near the May-apple.

"Is dat the Emperor guy?" asked Dogtick.

"No, Mr. Dogtick. This is a former aide to the Emperor Moth—Sergeant Thomas Hawkins, better known as 'the Hawk.' "

"Oh my gosh!" said Rosie.

The Hawk threw her a little salute.

"He's the one I told you about, sonny!" La Mère shouted. "The one I saw with that Mimi. They were embracing by the Lily Pond."

Jerking around to face La Mère, the Hawk fixed his eye on her and in a rasping, whispery voice said, "And what business is that of yours, madame?"

At the sound of the Hawk's voice, La Mère fluttered back in fright. Leon shivered. The Hawk had the voice of one who'd lived under a rock far too long.

"The Hawk, Rosie, and I all served together during the Mosquito Wars," said Spider Kane. "We were good friends until the Hawk became a hired soldier for the Emperor Moth."

"Why did you go work for him, Hawk?" said Rosie.

The Hawk smiled bitterly, then rasped, "I always preferred night work, Rosie. By the time I realized that night work with the Emperor meant crime and deceit, it was too late. By then I'd burrowed too deep into the dark."

"I hadn't seen the Hawk for ages," said Spider Kane. "But this morning, when I heard a deep cough near the May-apple, a shock of recognition went through me. It was the same dry hack that used to keep me awake nights in our tent. So I followed the retreating cough through the Wildflower Woods—until I found the Hawk hiding under a cold rock."

The moth nodded at Spider Kane. "And it's good to be with you again, Cap'n. And you too, Lieutenant Rose."

"Now, will you kindly tell us, Hawk, about the Emperor Moth?" said Spider Kane.

"The Emperor Moth is the emperor of the Dark Swamp," the Hawk rasped. "His island palace is no more than the rotting stump of a black ash. In spite of his riches, he chooses to live in wood rot and decay."

"How awful," said Little Pickles.

The Hawk shot a look at her. His eye burned with a horrid intensity. "He loves black, spongy earth, my lady. He loves leaf mold and fungus. He loves damp soil crawling with worms. He loves robber-flies and beetle grubs. He *loves* the underbelly of life."

"This goon's making me sick," said Colonel Appleworm.

The Hawk whirled around to face the colonel. "Yes, Colonel. I *was* a goon." He leaned forward menacingly. "I was the goon who silently crept into your flowerpot one dark night and stole your dear wife's precious purple scarf."

"Horrors!" said Midge. "Mr. Kane, you mean *this* creature was prowling about our home while Tubby and I slept?"

Colonel Appleworm pinched his wife for using his private nickname in public.

The Hawk threw back his head and laughed grotesquely. "Yes," he rasped, "yes, I was the goon who did it! I was the goon who crept about on tippytoes while you and Tubby slept. I was the goon who heard Tubby snoring as I plucked the scarf out of your fancy cedar-chip closet! I was the goon—"

"Ease up, Hawk," said Spider Kane.

"Sorry, Cap'n. Sorry." The Hawk pulled in his wings and bowed his head.

"I still don't understand. Why did you do these things, Hawk?" asked Rosie.

"Because I was a fool, Lieutenant Rose," said the Hawk in a hoarse and muffled voice. "I grew confused about the difference between right and wrong, and I did whatever the emperor ordered."

"Why did he order you to steal?"

The Hawk looked at Rosie. "Because the Emperor Moth loves to end each day with a crime. At dusk, he dresses in his maroon velvet suit and his white gloves. Then he gives his goons their orders for the evening. We go out and plunder the Ant Kingdom and Bee City—and the Flowerpot District of the well-to-do."

"Does the emperor himself go with you, Hawk?"

"Ha!" An angry smile crossed the Hawk's face. "The emperor seldom leaves the palace. But when he does, he always leaves his calling card at the scene of the crime—*The Emperor Moth Ends the Day*—"

"The message that was left near Mimi's burrow under the May-apple," Spider Kane said.

"But Mr. Kane!" cried Leon. "How come the emperor gave Mimi the stuff he stole? And why did he kidnap her?"

Spider Kane looked at Leon with sad and somber

eyes. "Because, Leon, your friend Mimi is the Emperor Moth's wife—the Empress of the Dark Swamp."

With a tiny groan, Leon fainted.

FOURTEEN

"Drink this, sweetie." Little Pickles gave Leon some water as the rest of the group whispered excitedly. Then Spider Kane helped him back into his seat.

"See, sonny!" said La Mère. "She wasn't only tacky, she was wicked!"

"Mrs. Leafwing," said Spider Kane. "I suggest you hold your judgments until you hear from my final guest."

As Spider Kane again stepped behind the pale leaf screen, Colonel Appleworm laughed out loud. "How in the world do they all fit back there, Midge?"

"Hush," said his wife.

A moment later, Spider Kane returned with a feeble gossamer-winged butterfly leaning on his arm.

Leon gave a start—the butterfly looked just like Mimi! She had beautiful, blue iridescent wings just like Mimi's. And her face was just like Mimi's, except for its deep, sad wrinkles.

"Perhaps Mimi's mother can help us understand," Spider Kane said. "Margaret?"

"One summer day a year ago, my daughter and I were in the woods sniffing flowers," the old butterfly began in a nasal, monotone voice. "Before I knew it, she was flitting away from me, looking for daffodils.

"As soon as she was out of my sight, I heard screaming. I flew as fast as I could. But when I came to a clearing, I saw a great winged creature flying into the air, carrying away my precious child. Her screams—still—echo—in my ears. . . ."

As the old butterfly hid her face and shook with sobs, Leon heard loud weeping elsewhere in the room. He turned and saw his mother waving her handkerchief dramatically. "Oh, that poor, poor mother!" she wailed.

"Empress Mimi was forced to share the Worm Wood Throne in the Hall of Decay, and she practically died of grief," rasped the Hawk.

La Mère sobbed louder. Dogtick patted her on the back sympathetically. "That poor, poor mother," repeated La Mère.

"Over time, as Mimi sat in the dimly lit, damp throne room, she nearly forgot her life in the sun," said the Hawk. "She grew thin and weak. But she always stayed kind. She smiled at me when I hadn't seen a smile in a long, long time." The Hawk looked away and took a deep breath. "So! I decided to help her escape. It was the first decent thing I'd done since I fought for Cap'n Kane."

Spider Kane nodded encouragingly. "Go on, Hawk," he said.

"Before Mimi went back to her mother, she wanted to return some of the emperor's stolen goods," said the Hawk. "So I brought her here to the Cottage Garden. After we hugged good-bye near the Lily Pond, I kept watch over her. Only"—the Hawk rolled his head back in anguish—"only I was sleeping when that monster came and—and—and caught—her—" The Hawk fell on the floor, convulsed with rage.

"But how did the emperor know where she was?" cried Leon.

Spider Kane stepped forward. "It seems that Mimi's first mission — returning the silk scarf to Mrs. Appleworm — was interrupted by the good intentions of a kind stranger, Leon. *You.* Soon the whole Garden was gossiping about your interest in her. The gossip spread until it reached the emperor himself."

"Argh!" Leon cried out. "It was *my* fault!" He fell beside the Hawk and beat his fists against the floor.

"Spy, do you think the emperor killed her?" said Rosie.

"No, Lieutenant Rose, I sincerely don't. My hunch is he expects Mimi to be his empress again. I imagine he enjoys forcing her to rule the Island of the Dark Swamp against her will. Only this time, I'm sure she's very well guarded."

"We must save her then!" cried Leon.

"Yeah, Cap'n!" croaked the Hawk.

"And help that poor mother!" wailed La Mère.

Spider Kane smiled. "I'm so glad we all agree, my friends. I've been quite restless since the Mosquito Wars ended."

Part III

FIFTEEN

"Mom?" said Leon, peeking into his mother's cracked geranium pot.

La Mère was packing her things, and Walter Dogtick was helping her. "You want to take this, Pupa?" Walter said, holding up her dandelion wig.

"Yep. Pack it up, lamb chop. It'll be good for a laugh someday," said La Mère.

Walter carefully put the dandelion wig into his old soiled sack.

"Mom?" said Leon. "What's going on?"

"I'm hittin' the road, sonny," said La Mère as she snapped a cheap strand of pop beads around her neck. "Those snobs at the Women's Bug Club won't have La Mère Leafwing to kick around anymore!"

"Where're you going?" said Leon.

"Back to the ole Goatweed Patch."

"Goatweed Patch?"

"Yep. I'm gonna take up residence in the empty chamber of an old wasp nest."

"But you always hated the Goatweed Patch," said Leon.

"Well, perhaps I don't hate it so much anymore, buster. At least the little buggies who live there don't go around with their noses stuck up in the air. And they don't run around falsely accusing one another, either." La Mère's lip trembled. Dogtick placed a comforting hand on her back. "And life must go on, huh, Wally?" she said.

"Dat's right, precious."

"And at least I have you."

"Dat's right, precious," said the old tick.

"So you two are good friends again?" said Leon.

La Mère grinned fondly at Dogtick. "The *best*," she said.

"I'm glad," Leon said, and he meant it.

Dogtick sighed. "Don't never say true love don't win out," he said to Leon.

"I hope you're right."

"You really care for that little butterfly, don't you, sonny?" said La Mère.

Leon nodded sadly.

"Well, I hope she turns up—for her mother's sake, of course. When do you characters leave on your little expedition?"

"At sundown we're meeting Spider Kane at the edge of the Garden," said Leon. "We'll sleep under the Honeysuckle Arch, then leave for the Dark Swamp and the emperor's island."

"Oh." La Mère stared at Leon as if she'd only just now become aware of the danger he was heading into. "Oh, honey," she gasped. "Don't let that ugly emperor grab you."

Leon laughed a little. "I won't, don't worry."

"I want you safe and—and happy, baby. Like what any good mother wants for her son."

"I know, I know," said Leon. He leaned over and kissed her. "I'm sorry I wrongly accused you," he whispered.

La Mère's eyes flooded with tears, and she sniffed. "Well, *you* I'll forgive. But not those horrible ex-friends of mine!" She let out a deep sob, then waved away her tears with a wing flutter and held her head up proudly. "Ready?" she said to Dogtick.

The grubby old tick nodded.

"Then climb on, lamb chop," she said.

Walter Dogtick climbed on La Mère's back, clutching his dirty sack to his chest.

"Good-bye, sonny!" La Mère called to Leon. "Tell that nasty emperor I'll kill him if he lays a hand on you!"

"Okay," said Leon, smiling.

La Mère threw him a kiss. Then she fluttered out of her cracked pot and carried Walter Dogtick away into the bright blue summer sky.

SIXTEEN

That evening when Leon arrived at the edge of the Garden, he found the others sitting around a small campfire, eating a dinner of crusty bread and roasted potatoes. Spider Kane, Rosie, Little Pickles, and the Hawk all looked quite amazing in the glow of the firelight.

Spider Kane wore his dark blue captain's uniform with a white glove on every hand, and he carried a canvas rucksack. Rosie wore her khaki-colored uniform. Little Pickles wore her reserve army uniform and carried a wicker picnic basket. And the Hawk wore a tattered gray jacket covered with tarnished medals.

Though they all greeted him warmly and offered him dinner, Leon felt very young and inexperienced next to them. He wore his bright green Bug Scout uniform, but it was too small. He tugged on his sleeves as he sat silently in the shadows and listened to the others plan the rescue mission.

"We'll get a good night's sleep here under the Honeysuckle Arch," said Spider Kane. He lit his pipe, then added, "At dawn, we'll move out of the Garden into the Forest."

"What route will we take, Spy?" asked Rosie.

"I've made a map," said Spider Kane. He reached into his rucksack, pulled out a tiny scrap of paper, and spread it on the ground in front of them.

Spider Kane traced their path with a white-gloved finger. "The Forest, the Dark Swamp, the emperor's island. We'll arrive at the Swamp by nightfall, then make our way to the palace in the dark."

❀   ❀   ❀

When the last light had faded from the sky, Spider Kane ordered them to turn in. "We have a long day ahead of us."

"Right, Cap'n," rasped the Hawk. "A long day — and night."

Spider Kane kept watch beside the fire while the others nestled down to sleep. Rosie and Little Pickles lay on small mats of woven grass, and the Hawk held his wings rooflike over his back.

As Leon looked up at the stars, he inhaled the sweet scent of the honeysuckle. He listened to Spider Kane tap his pipe against a log. He listened to peepers and bullfrogs calling from the Lily Pond. Just as he started to sink into sleep, a deep growling noise made him jump with fear. "What's that?" he cried.

Spider Kane chuckled. "Just the Hawk snoring," he said.

"Gracious," said Little Pickles.

Leon snuggled deeper into the grass and closed his eyes again. Suddenly the shrill cry of an unknown creature echoed in the distance. "What's that?" he said.

"It's the world outside the Garden, Leon," said Spider Kane in his deep, velvety voice.

Never in his life had Leon ventured outside the Cottage Garden. Suddenly the world on the other side of the stone wall seemed infinitely large and dangerous.

Leon lay down again and squeezed his eyes shut. As the wind rustled through the grass and weeds, he thought he heard whispers that said, *The Emperor Moth ends the day.*

Shivering in the damp darkness, Leon longed for warmth and daylight. He longed to see Mimi again. But the whisperings swelled in the breeze, saying, *The night is here to stay.*

SEVENTEEN

Leon woke just before dawn. The scent of chicory weed tea wafted through the air as gray light was beginning to filter through the lacy leaves overhead. As he stared up at the sky, he heard Spider

Kane's voice: "I like what I've seen so far," the spider said.

"I don't know, Spy," someone answered. It was a male voice Leon had never heard before. It was smooth and clear, nothing like the Hawk's rasping, throaty growl. "I still think he's too young. We wouldn't want anything to happen to a kid."

Leon jerked completely awake. Who was talking? And were they talking about him? He scrambled off the ground and flitted through the haze until he came upon the Hawk, Spider Kane, Rosie, and Little Pickles sitting near the campfire, sipping tea from acorn caps.

He quickly darted over to them. "Good morning," he said.

The Hawk cleared his throat and rasped, "Mornin', kid."

"Who was just here? I heard a strange voice," Leon said.

"Just us," said Rosie.

"Want some chicory weed tea, sweetie?" said Little Pickles.

93

Leon was confused. But at the moment he was more disturbed about *what* he had heard than about *who* had said it. Had they all been debating whether or not to take him along?

"Sure, I'll have some tea," said Leon. Actually he hated the bitter-tasting stuff. But this morning he'd force himself to drink it.

As Little Pickles poured more tea from a stone pot into an acorn cap, Spider Kane gave Leon a reassuring smile. "How'd you sleep?" he asked.

"Never better in my life," said Leon, though in fact he'd hardly slept at all.

"Good. Because today's probably going to be the longest day in your life," said Spider Kane.

"I've had longer," said Leon.

The spider nodded kindly, and Leon felt a bit ashamed for acting so defensive.

"Here you go, kid," the Hawk said as he passed the acorn cap.

"Leon. My name is Leon," said Leon.

"Good name," rasped the Hawk, giving him a crooked smile.

"When we start out, the Hawk and I will lead the way," said Spider Kane. "Then Rosie, then Little Pickles, and then Leon."

"I'm at the very end?" piped Leon before he could stop himself.

Spider Kane nodded. "I need you to guard against a rear attack."

Leon gulped. "Rear attack?"

"Hey, Cap'n, maybe you should give that job to Lieutenant Rose," said the Hawk.

"No, I want it," said Leon.

"This ain't no Bug Scouts, you know, Leon," rasped the Hawk. "It's a dangerous mission."

"I know that. I was the one who wanted to rescue Mimi in the first place, remember?"

"Calm down, Leon," said Spider Kane. "I think the Hawk is just worried that the emperor's henchmen may be patrolling the Forest."

"Yeah, his robber-flies," said the Hawk, "his assassin bugs, his mosquito commandos, his grubs, his—"

"Okay, honey," said Rosie. "We get the picture."

"Then if there're no more questions, let's be off," said Spider Kane.

The little army moved out of the Garden into the Forest, Spider Kane crawling with his slight limp alongside the low-flying Hawk. Behind him, Rosie and Little Pickles bumped through the air. Leon brought up the rear.

As he fluttered through the new world of the Forest, Leon's eyes darted from creeping vines and peeling bark to blackened roots and moss-covered rocks. Winding in and out among spindly saplings and furrowed gray tree trunks, he was terrified of caws and rustlings coming from the shadows.

Then to his horror a damp fog began to roll through the Forest. Soon all the trees and brush were blanketed in a thick white cloud.

Clickity click, click.

Leon looked about anxiously. The clicking noise was unlike other Forest sounds. But in the fog he couldn't see where it was coming from.

Clickity click, click.

Leon almost cried out for help, but he stopped himself. It was his job to protect the army from a rear attack.

Click, clickity click.

The clicking seemed to be coming from farther back in the Forest. Leon fluttered toward it, then stopped and waited.

The noise did not come again.

As Leon hovered in the ghostly vapor, he felt as if he were being watched by unseen eyes. The Forest seemed strangely still, and the air felt cold and clammy. He shivered, then turned and began hurrying back to find the others.

But Leon was lost. He couldn't find his friends in the fog. "Rosie! Little Pickles! Mr. Kane!" he cried. He was certain something was following him. As he tried to escape, he flew into sticky webs and grasping vines. He banged into trees and fallen limbs. Battered and bruised, he screamed, "Help! Help!"

Just when Leon thought he was going to die of terror, four white-gloved hands reached out of the gloom.

Leon beat his wings frantically as Spider Kane grabbed him.

"Be still," the spider said, holding him tightly. "Be still."

EIGHTEEN

"Fear is a trickster, Leon," said Spider Kane. "You must banish him before he tricks you into a panic. Only then can you solve the problem at hand."

Leon was still so frightened he could barely speak.

"How'd you lose us, Leafy?" said Rosie.

"I thought I heard something behind me," Leon mumbled, "so I went to check on it."

"What did it sound like?" asked Spider Kane.

"It was some sort of clicking noise."

"*Clicking* noise?" Spider Kane ran a hand over his face.

The Hawk groaned. "Are you thinkin' what I'm thinkin', Cap'n?"

Spider Kane nodded silently.

"What are you thinking?" cried Leon.

"Deathwatch beetles," whispered Spider Kane.

Leon stopped breathing.

"Tapping a telegraph message to the emperor," rasped the Hawk. "Telling him about us."

"Oh no!" Leon burst into tears. He couldn't help himself.

"Oh, don't cry, Leon," pleaded Little Pickles. "Everything's okay. It's not what you think! We're all just—"

"Little Pickles!" interrupted Rosie. "What are you saying?"

"We're all just—what?" cried Leon.

Little Pickles looked as if she'd suddenly swallowed a gnat. "I—I just meant that things usually work out for the best, don't they, Rosie?"

"Sure they do," said Rosie. Then she turned to Leon. "Are you all right, Leafy?"

"Yes, yes, I'm fine," Leon gasped as he dried his eyes on his Bug Scout sleeve. "I'm sorry. I just—I just lost control. . . ."

"It happens to all of us, Leon," said Spider Kane kindly. "Come on, let's get—"

"Wait! Shhh!" said the Hawk. "Listen!"

Leon's heart caught in his throat as he listened to an eerie whining sound coming from the distance. He couldn't see through the fog, but the noise was growing louder and louder.

"Aw, nuts!" said the Hawk.

"Mosquito patrol!" said Spider Kane. "Hide! Hide!"

They all scattered into the mist. Leon, Rosie, and Little Pickles scooted into a curled brown oak leaf. As the whining noise grew louder and louder, Leon trembled inside the musty-smelling tunnel and whispered to his pounding heart, "Be still, be still."

Finally the terrible sound faded away.

When they heard the Hawk coughing, Leon, Rosie, and Little Pickles crept slowly out of the curled leaf.

"They'll be back," said Spider Kane. "They won't give up. Let's move, *fast.*"

The fog began to lift as Leon fluttered quickly behind Rosie and Little Pickles. Still he jumped at every sound—at every cough of the Hawk, every *snap* of a breaking twig, every *chur* of a snowy tree cricket.

Several times he hit the ground and held his breath when the terrible wing whine of the mosquitos sounded from the distance. But each time, the whirring patrol moved on.

Finally in the late afternoon the little army left the Forest and began climbing a weedy slope at the edge of the Dark Swamp. The weeds were so thick and high that Leon could barely see his friends as they preceded him up the hill. But suddenly he heard Spider Kane utter, "Good heavens!"

Leon zoomed to the crest of the hill. Squeezing between Rosie and Little Pickles, he peered down at the shore and saw a sight he would not forget for the rest of his life.

NINETEEN

A huge, wriggling mass was moving across the sandbank of the Dark Swamp.

"How awful!" breathed Little Pickles.

"What are they doing, Spy?" said Rosie.

"Military exercises," said Spider Kane.

For the first time, Leon realized the writhing mass was a horde of grubs. He couldn't speak or move as he stared at the hideous army parading up and down the sandbank.

"We'll never get past them alive, Spy," said Rosie.

"She's right, Cap'n," said the Hawk.

Spider Kane turned to Leon. "What do you think?" he said.

Leon was shocked that Spider Kane even cared what he thought. "Um, I think we can do it," he said, trying to sound brave.

"Ah, kid, you don't know these guys," rasped the Hawk.

But Spider Kane kept staring at Leon. "Tell us, son," he said. "How do you think we can get past them to rescue Mimi?"

Mimi. Just the sound of her name made Leon ache. He would do anything to save her. "Maybe we can fly," he said.

"That's fine for you and me, kid," said the Hawk. "But the ladybugs are a bit slow and the Cap'n's earthbound."

"Well, what if you carry Rosie and Little Pickles? And I'll carry Mr. Kane," said Leon.

"Nah, kid, he's twice your size," said the Hawk.

"Maybe I can hang from you by one of my cobweb threads, Leon," said Spider Kane. "You want to try it?"

"Yes, sir."

"Good." Spider Kane took a ball of cobweb from his rucksack. He snipped off a short filament and lashed the end of it to Leon's Bug Scout sash.

"There," he said. "Now, Rosie, Little Pickles, climb on the Hawk's back." When they were ready to go, Spider Kane saluted them. Then the Hawk took off into the twilight, carrying the two ladybugs.

"All right, Leon," said Spider Kane. "Follow the Hawk and fly as high and swiftly as you can."

As Leon lifted off the ground, Spider Kane swung beneath him like a kite in the wind. Leon rocked from side to side and almost flipped over. But he steadied himself, then fluttered higher and higher after the Hawk—until he and Spider Kane sailed unnoticed over the emperor's wretched army.

Then, suddenly, the most extraordinary thing happened. Leon thought he saw Mimi in the distance. She was fluttering toward the emperor's island, her blue wings shining in the fleeting gray light.

Was his fear playing another trick on him? "MIMI!" he screamed. And in the twilight, from far away, the mysterious vision seemed to turn and look at him with an expression of utter horror.

Suddenly Spider Kane jerked so hard on his cobweb thread that Leon somersaulted through the air. When he finally steadied himself again, night had cloaked the stream in darkness, and his vision of Mimi had vanished.

TWENTY

"It looked just like her," Leon was explaining to the group as they huddled together in the marsh grass at the edge of the island.

"Sometimes in the twilight our deepest dreams and wishes shimmer before our eyes," said Spider Kane. "But what you saw, Leon, was not a gossamer-winged butterfly. It was a violet damselfly. I saw her too."

"Are you sure? Maybe Mimi escaped from the emperor's palace," said Leon.

"Look! There it is," said the Hawk.

The moon was peeking out from behind a cloud. And now in the dim light, the group could see the silhouette of the rotting stump of a black ash.

"That's where Mimi really is, Leon," whispered Spider Kane.

As Leon stared at the monstrous palace, his vision of Mimi faded into the gloom. He felt sick now, imagining her trapped inside the black stump.

"During the night, the blue lamps of glowworms light the winding corridors," the Hawk said in a terrible whisper. "One passageway leads to the Hall of Decay. Another to a dungeon filled with the claws and wings of the traitors the emperor has starved to death."

"Oh my," said Little Pickles. "What wickedness."

"Yes, and wickedness longs to entwine itself with goodness, Little Pickles," said Spider Kane. "That's why the emperor wants to keep Mimi as his queen."

"I don't care why he wants to keep her. We've got to save her!" said Leon.

"Cool down, kid," rasped the Hawk. "Or you'll be joining those bug parts in the dungeon."

"This is the plan," said Spider Kane. "I want the three of you to wait here while the Hawk and I head into the palace."

"Can't I go with you?" asked Leon.

"Don't worry, Leon. We need your help, but later," said Spider Kane. "First we have to split into two regiments. The Hawk is going to guide me through a secret tunnel that leads to the royal chambers where the emperor and Mimi sleep.

"As we travel through the palace, I'll spin a thread for the three of you. Once we're safely hiding inside an empty gallery, I'll tug on the thread. Follow it. When you join us, we'll rescue Mimi together."

"But what if his guards see your thread? This won't work! What if they capture you? I don't understand," said Leon.

"Oh Leafy, soon it will all make sense," said Little Pickles.

"Let's just do what Spy says," said Rosie.

"Trust me, Leon," said Spider Kane. He reached into his rucksack and took out his ball of cobweb thread. Then he handed Leon the end. "When you feel a strong tug, follow the thread to the palace."

"C'mon, Cap'n, we can go now!" said the Hawk. "The blue lamps are comin' on. They'll be heading for bed."

"Wait," said Leon. "I still don't understand. What if—"

"Be brave," whispered Spider Kane to him. Then he and the Hawk crept away into the night.

"But what if they get caught?" Leon said.

"During the Mosquito Wars, Spy captured whole armies by throwing cobweb nets over them," whispered Rosie. "And the Hawk can do anything."

"He's a brilliant actor," said Little Pickles.

"What do you mean—a brilliant actor?" said Leon.

"Oh, I just mean he seems to be quite clever," said Little Pickles.

A memory of the early morning came back to Leon. "When I woke up," he said, "I heard a voice that didn't sound like the Hawk or Spider Kane. Who was talking?"

"Oh, I have no idea, Leafy," said Rosie. "The morning seems a million years away."

"Yes, it's all quite a blur to me," said Little Pickles.

Clouds scudded across the moon, and the wind moaned. As Leon stared in silence at the dark palace, he felt very alone. For some reason, he no longer completely trusted Rosie and Little Pickles. Everyone in the group seemed to know things he didn't.

Suddenly Leon felt a tug on the thread. "Hey!" he cried, "let's go!"

"But it's too soon!" cried Rosie.

Then the thread was jerked from Leon's hands. He yelped. "Oh no! It's gone!"

"Gone?"

"It got yanked away! Something happened!" Suddenly all Leon wanted to do was fly home.

"Maybe Spy fell or something," said Rosie.

"Oh no, then he's hurt," said Leon.

"No, no, I don't think so," said Rosie. "Spiders never get hurt when they fall."

Leon's mind suddenly leaped to a faraway time and place. "What falls down and never gets hurt?" he asked the night.

"What?" said Rosie.

"Snow," he answered softly, and he remembered

her lovely laugh, her little song, and her dance, and he moaned with sorrow.

"Leafy? What's wrong?"

"I almost forgot her," he whispered. "Mimi." He looked at Rosie. "I have to save Mimi, no matter what. I'm going into the palace."

"We'll go with you!" said Rosie.

"Good. Climb on my back."

Rosie and Little Pickles hoisted themselves onto Leon. Then the three of them took off through the moonless dark, headed for the emperor's palace.

TWENTY-ONE

The stench of decay filled the air as Leon, Rosie, and Little Pickles lit down at the base of the black ash stump.

"Where's the entrance?" whispered Leon.

"There's a blue light," said Rosie, pointing to a glowworm lamp. It was shining inside a crumbling hole that was nearly covered with peeling bark. "I'll go in there. Then you two follow me. Count to ten before you come."

"Wait," said Leon, his courage starting to leave him. "Let's stay together."

"We can't. We should go one at a time," said Rosie. "If one of us gets caught, the others can come to the rescue. I'll go first. Then Little Pickles. Then you."

"Wait, wait," whispered Leon. But before he could say anything more, Rosie crept into the stump.

"This is crazy," Leon said to Little Pickles. "We need more of a plan."

But the ladybug wasn't listening. "Eight, nine, ten," she whispered, then vanished into the stump after Rosie.

"Little Pick—!" Leon said, but it was too late. He was all alone.

Suddenly a scream came from inside the palace. It sounded like Rosie! Then another scream—Little Pickles! Then there was silence.

But the screams echoed in Leon's ears as if the very night were screaming. Unbearably afraid, he fluttered off the ground and hovered in the dark. Half of him was desperate to escape the terror inside the palace. The other half was overwhelmed with fury and determination.

The rising wind whispered, *Escape! Escape!*

But Leon said, "No!" And he darted to the entrance of the hollow stump and crept into the emperor's palace.

The blue glowworm lamps lit the vestibule of the palace. Numerous black tunnels spread like veins around the curved, worm-eaten walls. Leon saw no signs of anyone—not his friends, not the emperor, not the emperor's guards.

But then he heard music—clear, melancholy strains coming from a higher level in the stump. It sounded as if Spider Kane were playing his clarinet. Perhaps the emperor was forcing the spider to entertain him while his friends were being tortured.

Rage pushed Leon down the winding tunnel that led to the clarinet sounds. The music grew louder and louder as he crawled along the dank-smelling worm-eaten wood, then passed through empty galleries lit by dim blue lights.

The music ceased just as Leon fluttered into a large hollow space. It was a dead end. Looking wildly about the chamber, he still saw no signs of grub guards or robber-flies. No signs of Little Pickles, Rosie, the Hawk, or Spider Kane. And no signs of Mimi or the Emperor Moth.

"Rosie?" he whispered frantically. "Little Pickles?"

Silence.

Leon's fear began to turn into panic. He felt close to fainting, but he clenched his fists. "No! No!" he whispered fiercely. Then he took a deep breath. And as he let the air out slowly, a calm and deadly anger banished the trickster within him. For the first time in his life, he felt absolutely sure of himself. *"Emperor!"* he called.

Silence.

"Emperor Moth, come out here! Where are you?" His voice now shook with rage.

"Here."

Leon jerked around as a spindly figure stepped from the shadows. "I'm here, Leon," he said.

"Mr. Kane!" cried Leon. "Where's everyone else? Where's the Emperor Moth?"

"Here," said Spider Kane. On his thin lips was a smile.

"Where?" said Leon, looking about.

"Here," said Spider Kane.

"Where?"

"*I* am the Emperor Moth," said Spider Kane.

TWENTY-TWO

"*You?*"

"Yes."

"*You* are the Emperor Moth?"

"Yes."

"Wh-what do you mean?"

"The Emperor Moth is my code name," said Spider Kane.

Leon stepped back. Spider Kane looked larger than before. His voice sounded deeper. And in the light of the blue lamps, his face had an expression of deadly seriousness.

"Your—your code name?" Leon felt as if he couldn't breathe.

"I'm the commander of a secret band called the Order of the MOTH, Leon."

The wind whistled eerily through the dark stump. "Wh-what's that?"

"Before I explain, allow me to introduce my most trusted lieutenants."

Out of the shadows stepped Rosie, Little Pickles, and the Hawk.

"What's going on?" breathed Leon.

"Now let me introduce one other lieutenant," said Spider Kane.

Mimi entered the hall, carrying a blue lamp.

Leon laughed a short hysterical laugh. This was a dream, a crazy nightmare that was rolling over him just as the fog had rolled through the Forest earlier.

But Spider Kane looked very real in the cold, blue light. "We are all members of the Order of the MOTH," he said. "Recently Rosie and Little Pickles urged me to make you a member also. They've watched you grow up. And they claimed that you were strong and dependable. I believed that you were still too young to join us. However, we all finally agreed to send you on a quest. The journey had to be very difficult. For someday, we all might have to place our lives in your hands."

"I'm sorry I couldn't tell you the truth, Leafy," said Rosie.

"I was dying to tell you," said Little Pickles.

"You almost did," said Rosie.

Leon felt dizzy. The wind blew harder than ever, and the blue lights made his head swirl.

"Allow me to introduce you to Thomas Hawkins," said Spider Kane. "The greatest living actor of the moth world."

"Welcome to the emperor's palace, Leon," said the Hawk in a smooth, soft voice. Then he pulled off his eye patch and red bandanna.

"You played your part perfectly, Hawk," said Spider Kane. "And so did you, Leon. Don't think for a moment Mimi wasn't aware that you and your mother were watching her when she dropped the scarf."

"Does—does my mother know about this?" Leon said, trembling.

"Oh my, no. I must say her untimely threats nearly upset our whole plan. She and the innocent Mr.

Dogtick stumbled into our little drama quite unex-
pectedly."

"And then I nearly ruined everything by getting
here too late," said Mimi. "I almost died when I saw
you flying over the water!"

Leon stared at Mimi. "So—so you were never the
empress of the Dark Swamp?"

"No, I'm just a part-time actress Spy once directed
in a production of *Bug's Delight.*"

"I guess—I guess you thought I was an idiot then,"
Leon stammered. He looked at Mimi with a stricken
expression. "You must have had a great laugh when
you told them about my fear of h-having skinny arms,
and my singing, and they must have all laughed about
the fact that I liked you—a lot!"

Before anyone could say anything, Leon turned and
fluttered blindly away from the group. He rushed
down the dank-smelling black tunnel and through the
worm-eaten wood galleries. He crashed into peeling
bark and crumbling walls until finally he arrived at
the jagged entrance of the stump.

As he staggered outside, the cool wind and grass
seemed to be laughing at him.

Leon shivered in the moonlight, until he froze at the sound of the deep, velvety voice behind him.

"You can't escape us, Leon," said Spider Kane.

"Leave me alone," said Leon, his teeth chattering. "I'm not as d-dumb as you think. I knew something was f-fishy. I heard a strange voice at the campsite, remember? And I said I saw Mimi, re-remember? I saw her, but you tried to make me think I was d-dreaming!"

"Leon, listen. This wasn't mere fun at your expense," said Spider Kane. "It was a deadly serious quest. It was the only way the Order of the MOTH could discover the answers to many important questions."

"Wh-what questions?"

Rosie's voice bounced from the cold dark: "In spite of his young age, could Leon Leafwing navigate the world outside the Cottage Garden?"

Then came Little Pickles: "If Leon Leafwing lost his leader, would he still continue the quest?"

And the Hawk: "Would Leon push his way past terrible fear, wood rot, mold, and decay to save his friends?"

And Mimi: "And Leon Leafwing answered *yes, yes, yes* to all those questions. . . ." She fluttered close to Leon and whispered, "And I never laughed at him. I loved him from the first moment I stared into his eyes."

Then Spider Kane spoke. "Leon, you went on a journey to find the Emperor Moth and to be with Mimi again. You have succeeded in both. But most important, along the way you found what you were truly looking for—*your own strength and courage.*"

Leon turned to the five silhouettes standing before him in the early dawn light.

"Will you join us?" said Spider Kane.

"But what do you do?" said Leon.

"The Order of the MOTH is a secret band of bugs I formed after the Mosquito Wars," said Spider Kane. "Our purpose is to help those who are unable to help themselves. The initials M-O-T-H stand for Mission: Only to Help. We save water striders from flash floods and crickets from brush fires. We feed and educate orphaned ants. We find shelter for hiveless bees. We solve mysteries and fight injustice wherever we find it."

"Are there any other members?"

"Only the five of us," said Spider Kane.

"But what about Dr. Ant and Major General Bum?"

"Right here, lad," the Hawk said in Dr. Ant's falsetto. Then he saluted and hummed like General Bum, "Hmmmmm."

"You were *both* those guys?" said Leon.

"Mmm-hmm," said the Hawk.

"That explains why you were all wearing the same Italian shoes."

"Whoops," said the Hawk.

"You have a good eye, Leon," said Spider Kane, chuckling. "Now let me introduce you to Mimi's mother, Margaret."

"Thank you for finding my precious daughter, Leon," said Mimi in the nasal voice of the old butterfly.

"You?" Leon was truly stunned.

"Yes," said Mimi.

"And the so-called Ant Trilogy was merely three battered, second-rate novels Mimi really did find at a flea market," said Spider Kane. "And she found her rhinestone crown at the Bee City Thrift Store.

"The only robbery that actually occurred was the 'borrowing' of Midge Appleworm's scarf by Rosie. Since Midge has over two hundred silk scarves, we hoped she wouldn't be too much inconvenienced."

Leon gasped. He could hardly believe the enormity of the drama they had staged for his sake. "But what about all the other things that happened? The clicking noises?" he said.

"It's that time of year when deathwatch beetles click out their mating calls," said Spider Kane.

"But the mosquito patrols?"

"You can always count on mosquitoes being in the Forest in the summer," said Thomas Hawkins.

"What about the grub army?" Asked Leon.

Spider Kane chuckled. "I merely coordinated our arrival at the stream with the annual Grub Day Parade."

Leon shook his head in astonishment.

"Good heavens, Leon," said Spider Kane. "Did you really think I knew the head size of a gossamer-winged butterfly?"

Leon began to laugh. He couldn't believe Spider Kane and the others had gone to so much trouble just for him. As he laughed, Mimi slipped her hand into his. And the dawn wind felt softer and warmer.

"Will you join us, Leon?" said Spider Kane.

"Yes," breathed Leon. "Yes. Yes. Yes."

"Sure you want to fly with us, kid?" said the Hawk. "We've got some pretty dangerous adventures ahead."

"I'm flying," said Leon.

"Good, very good," said Spider Kane. Then he tightened one of the gloves on his hands. "Well, then, I must leave all of you now. I have some appointments to keep. But soon I'll return and gather you together."

"What do I do next?" piped Leon.

"Go back to the Cottage Garden with the others," said Spider Kane. "Relax. Celebrate. Then get ready."

"Ready?"

"Yes, Lieutenant Leafwing," said Spider Kane in his deep, velvety voice. "This has only been the beginning."

"Yes, sir," whispered Leon.

Spider Kane smiled. Then he threw a little salute to all of them and began crawling away. With his slight limp, he moved jerkily over the wet island grass.

"How will he get across the Dark Swamp?" asked Leon.

"Oh, there's plenty of bugs by the wharves—water boatmen and backswimmers," said Rosie. "One of them will carry him across. Spider Kane has friends everywhere."

In silence Leon and the others watched their mysterious commander disappear into the blinding light of the rising sun.

MARY POPE OSBORNE is a first-rate storyteller and the author of numerous works of fiction and nonfiction for all ages. Her books for Knopf include *Moonhorse, A Visit to Sleep's House, American Tall Tales,* and *Spider Kane and the Mystery at Jumbo Nightcrawler's*, a sequel to *Spider Kane and the Mystery Under the May-Apple.*

Ms. Osborne lives with her husband, Will, in New York City.

VICTORIA CHESS is a highly acclaimed illustrator of children's books, including *A Hippopotamusn't* by J. Patrick Lewis and *Tales for a Perfect Child* by Florence Parry Heide. A gardener, she found creepy inspiration for these illustrations right in her own backyard.

Ms. Chess lives in Connecticut with her husband, Ben, her son, Sam, and their two dogs and three cats.